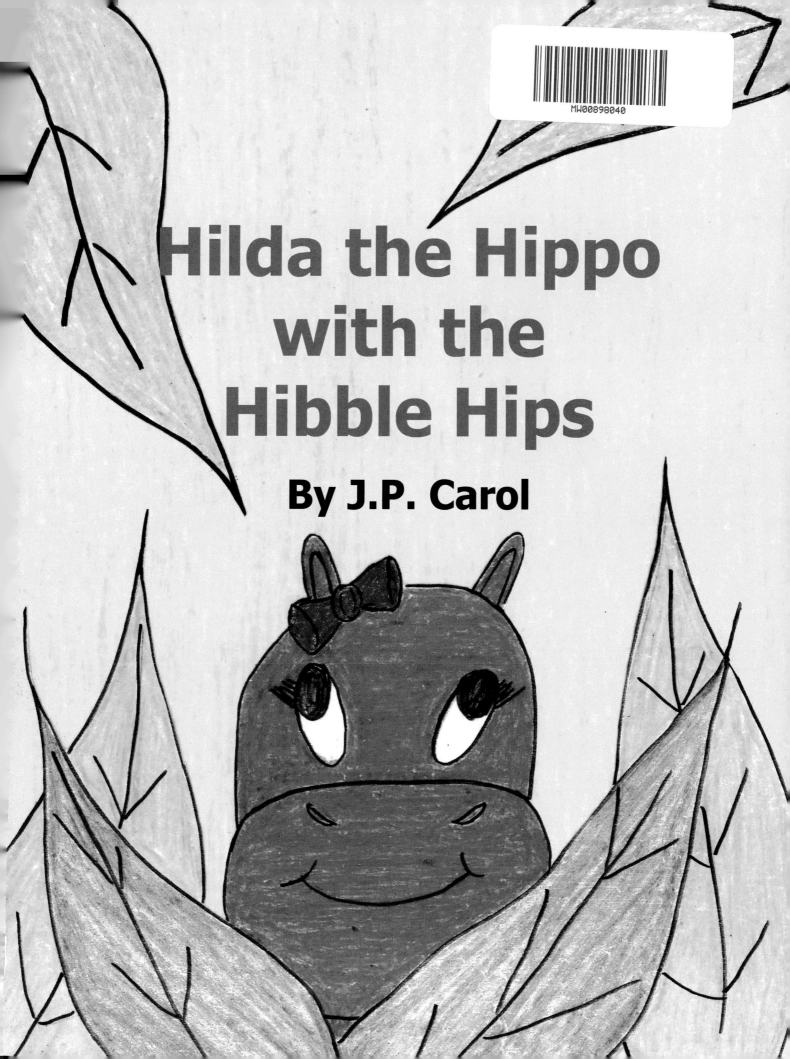

Hilda the Hippo with the Hibble Hips

By J.P. Carol

ISBN: 1475267134

ISBN-13: 9781475267136

To my loving nephews, Caleb, Isaiah and Jayden.

I love you always. This book is for you.

Your Auntie J.

BRISSSSSH! BOOM! BOOM! BOOM!
BRISSSSSH! BOOM!
DO YOU KNOW WHAT THAT SOUND IS?
THAT'S THE SOUND OF HILDA THE HIPPO WITH
THE HIBBLE HIPS — DANCING IN THE MIDDLE OF THE
JUNGLE.
AND WHEN SHE DANCES, SHE HAS ONE ARM UP
IN THE AIR WITH HER FINGER SHAKING TO A BEAT THAT
ONLY SHE CAN HEAR.
AND EVERYTIME SHE WIGGLED HER HIPS AND DANCED,
THE JUNGLE SHOOK, AND.....
BRISSSSSH! BOOM!
ANOTHER TREE WOULD FALL!
YOU SEE. EVEN THOUGH HILDA WAS A HIPPO, SHE
LOVED TO DANCE.

ONE HOT, SUNNY DAY,
HILDA HEARD HER FRIENDS
LAUGHING AND PLAYING
AT THE POND.
THEY WERE HAVING SO
MUCH FUN, THAT
HILDA DECIDED
TO JOIN THEM.
SHE CLIMBED TO THE TOP OF THE
ROCK ABOVE THE POND, AND
JUMPED INTO
THE COOL WATER BELOW.
AND AS HILDA JUMPED, SHE
YELLED…
"LOOK OUT BELOW! HERE I COME!"
ALL OF THE OTHER JUNGLE
ANIMALS RAN FOR COVER.
THEY WERE AFRAID TO WATCH.
THEN THEY HEARD IT!
SPLASSSSSH!! SWOSSSSSH!!
PLOPPPPP!!

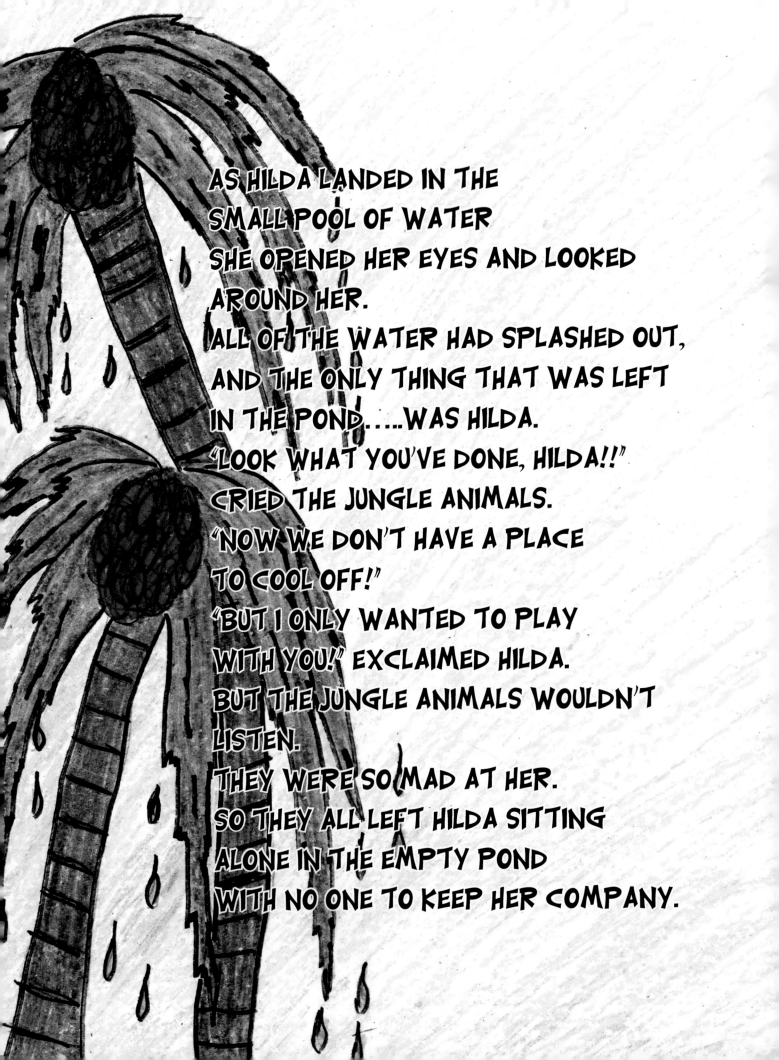

AS HILDA LANDED IN THE
SMALL POOL OF WATER
SHE OPENED HER EYES AND LOOKED
AROUND HER.
ALL OF THE WATER HAD SPLASHED OUT,
AND THE ONLY THING THAT WAS LEFT
IN THE POND.....WAS HILDA.
"LOOK WHAT YOU'VE DONE, HILDA!!"
CRIED THE JUNGLE ANIMALS.
"NOW WE DON'T HAVE A PLACE
TO COOL OFF!"
"BUT I ONLY WANTED TO PLAY
WITH YOU!" EXCLAIMED HILDA.
BUT THE JUNGLE ANIMALS WOULDN'T
LISTEN.
THEY WERE SO MAD AT HER.
SO THEY ALL LEFT HILDA SITTING
ALONE IN THE EMPTY POND
WITH NO ONE TO KEEP HER COMPANY.

ONE DAY, AS HILDA WAS EATING HER USUAL LUNCH OF DAISIES AND DAFFODILS AND SUNFLOWERS AND SUCH, SHE DECIDED TO SIT DOWN ON A ROCK.
"AHHH!" SAID HILDA AS SHE SAT DOWN.
"IT FEELS SO GOOD!"
BUT HILDA DIDN'T KNOW THAT BUMBLE THE BEE WAS ALREADY SITTING ON THE ROCK.

THEN ALL OF A SUDDEN, HILDA YELLED.
"EEEOOW!! OOOH!! OOOH!! OOOH!! EEEOOW!!"
YOU SEE, BUMBLE THE BEE DIDN'T LIKE BEING SAT ON.
HILDA JUMPED AND WIGGLED AND SQUIRMED AND
SQUIGGLED ALL THROUGH THE JUNGLE, WITH BUMBLE
THE BEE STUCK ON HER HIP. AS HILDA RAN, TREES FELL
TO THE LEFT AND TREES FELL TO THE RIGHT.

BUT ONCE AGAIN, THE JUNGLE ANIMALS
WERE MAD AT HILDA.
"THAT DOES IT!" THEY SAID.
"YOU MUST LEAVE THE JUNGLE,
HILDA!"
"YOUR DANCING MAKES SO
MUCH NOISE, IT'S TERRIBLE!"
SAID GERALD THE GIRAFFE. "I CAN'T
SLEEP!"
"AND WE WON'T HAVE ANY TREES TO
CLIMB IF YOU KEEP KNOCKING THEM OVER!" SAID
MILDRED THE MONKEY.
"AND NOW BECAUSE OF YOU, WHEN IT GETS
HOT, WE DON'T HAVE A PLACE TO SWIM
ANYMORE!" SAID ELBERT THE ELEPHANT.
"BESIDES, HIPPOS AREN'T SUPPOSED TO
DANCE!" GRUFFED LEO THE LION.
HILDA WAS SO SAD. SHE DIDN'T WANT TO LEAVE HER
FRIENDS.
"BUT I WASN'T DANCING," SHE SAID. "BUMBLE THE BEE
STUNG ME, AND I WAS TRYING TO SHAKE HIM OFF! IT
HURT SO BAD!"
BUT NOBODY WOULD BELIEVE HER.

SO HILDA LEFT THE JUNGLE BECAUSE HER FRIENDS DIDN'T WANT HER TO DANCE ANYMORE. SHE WAS SAD AND LONELY.

AS HILDA SAT ALL BY HERSELF ON HER FAVORITE ROCK, SHE HUNG HER HEAD AS BIG TEARS FELL FROM HER EYES.

THE VERY NEXT DAY,
IT STARTED TO RAIN.
IT RAINED AND IT RAINED. IT RAINED
SO HARD, HILDA THOUGHT IT
WOULD NEVER STOP!
SHE JUMPED ON TOP OF HER FAVORITE ROCK
AS THE WATER STARTED TO RISE AROUND HER.
THE RIVER THAT RAN THROUGH THE JUNGLE GOT
BIGGER AND BIGGER.
"OH MY GOSH!!" CRIED HILDA. "IT'S GOING TO
FLOOD THE JUNGLE! I'VE GOT TO WARN
MY FRIENDS!"

THE OTHER ANIMALS WERE AFRAID AND DIDN'T KNOW WHAT TO DO OR WHERE TO HIDE.
THEY HAD NEVER SEEN IT RAIN SO HARD BEFORE.
THEN ALL OF A SUDDEN, THEY HEARD A SOUND IN THE JUNGLE.
BRISSSSSSH!! BOOM!! BOOM!! BOOM!!
BRISSSSSSH!! BOOM!!
DO YOU KNOW WHAT THAT SOUND IS?

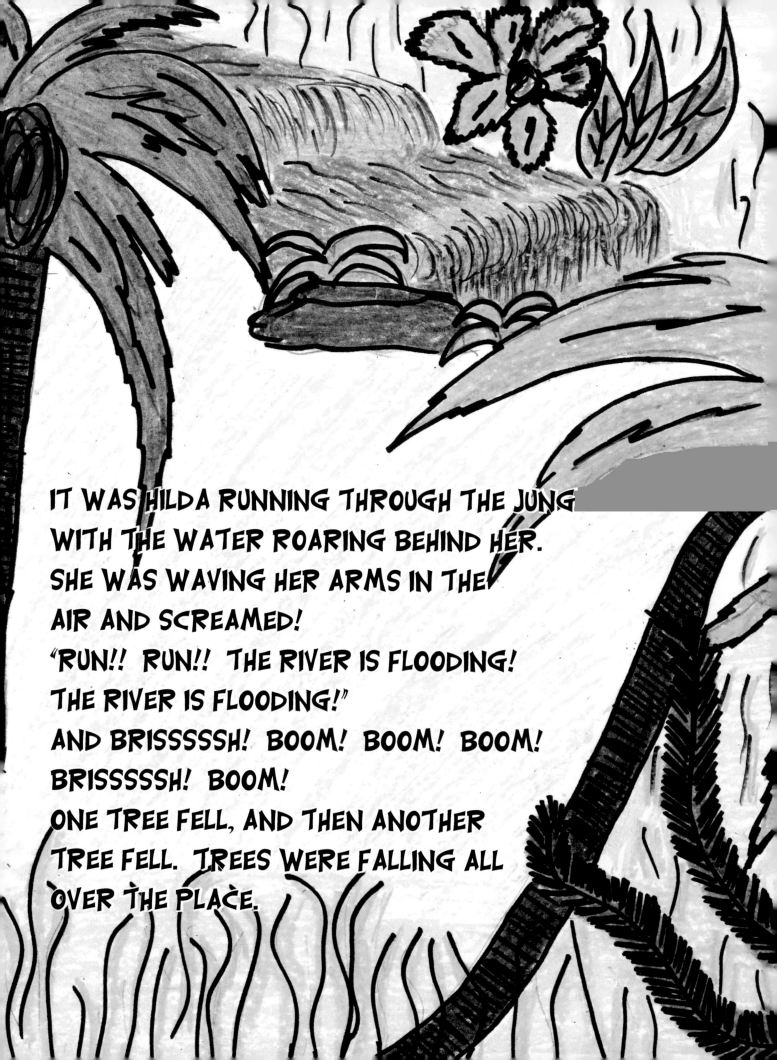

IT WAS HILDA RUNNING THROUGH THE JUNGLE
WITH THE WATER ROARING BEHIND HER.
SHE WAS WAVING HER ARMS IN THE
AIR AND SCREAMED!
"RUN!! RUN!! THE RIVER IS FLOODING!
THE RIVER IS FLOODING!"
AND BRISSSSSH! BOOM! BOOM! BOOM!
BRISSSSSH! BOOM!
ONE TREE FELL, AND THEN ANOTHER
TREE FELL. TREES WERE FALLING ALL
OVER THE PLACE.

HILDA SHOOK THE GROUND SO HARD, THAT AS THE
TREES FELL, THEY STOPPED THE WATER FROM
FLOODING THE JUNGLE.
AND WHEN THE RAIN FINALLY STOPPED, HILDA LOOKED
AROUND.
SHE WAS SO HAPPY THAT HER FRIENDS WERE SAFE,
AND THEIR JUNGLE HOME HAD BEEN SAVED.

SO THE OTHER JUNGLE ANIMALS GAVE HILDA A PARTY TO THANK HER FOR SAVING THEM AND THEIR JUNGLE HOME.

THEY WERE SORRY THAT THEY HAD BEEN MEAN TO HILDA, AND HAD ASKED HER TO LEAVE THE JUNGLE.

THEY REALIZED THAT HILDA WAS JUST BEING HERSELF. AND THAT BEING DIFFERENT WAS OKAY!

SO THEY ALL PUT ON THEIR PARTY HATS AND DANCED AROUND HILDA. AND THEY TOLD HER THAT SHE COULD DANCE ANYTIME SHE WANTED TO. AS LONG AS SHE NEVER CHANGED.

Made in the USA
Middletown, DE
23 April 2022